But still . . .

In five days, Kathy Kerrigan was supposed to get married. It would be the social wedding of the year. She and Brad planned to exchange their vows at St. Patrick's Cathedral, then host a lavish reception at Tavern on the Green and finally head off for a month-long European honeymoon. The beginning of a wonderful new life for the two of them. A chance, finally, to bury the memories of the past.

But, as she sat there, with the past staring back at her from the TV screen, Kathy knew that some memories simply cannot be buried.

There was no choice for her—she had to go back.

Back to the time when she was a little girl again.

Back down the tangled trail of memories she hoped would somehow lead to the answers of what really happened that day twenty years before that had changed her life so irrevocably.

And back to wherever that trail might lead her.